WALTER'S
Wonderful
WEB

tim hopgood

MACMILLAN CHILDREN'S BOOKS

Walter wished he could spin
a perfect web, just like his friends.

WALTER'S *Wonderful* WEB

First published 2015 by Macmillan Children's Books
This edition published 2017 by Macmillan Children's Books
an imprint of Pan Macmillan,
20 New Wharf Road, London N1 9RR
Associated companies throughout the world
www.panmacmillan.com

ISBN: 978-1-5098-3021-3

9 8 7 6 5 4 3 2 1

A CIP catalogue record for this book is available from the British Library.

Printed in China

But Walter's webs weren't perfect.

They were wibbly-wobbly.

And when the wind blows,
wibbly-wobbly webs always blow away!

But Walter was determined. So one morning he decided to start with something simple.

Very carefully he made a
small web in the shape of a . . .

Triangle.

Whoosh! went the wind
and it blew the web away.

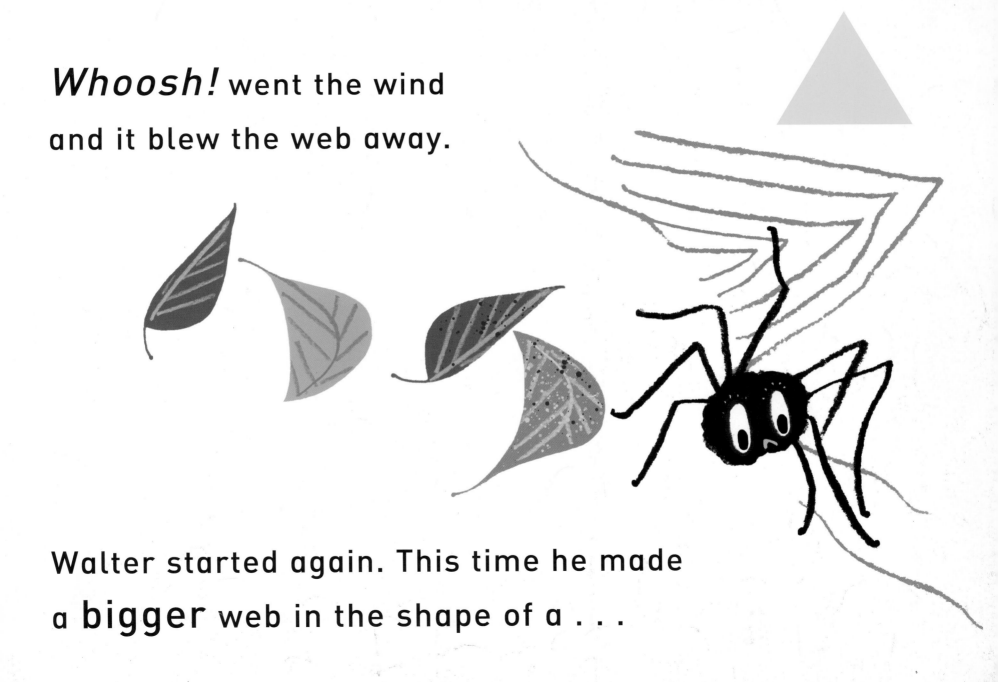

Walter started again. This time he made
a **bigger** web in the shape of a . . .

Square.

Whoosh! went the wind

and it blew the web away.

Walter sighed and started again.

This time he made a longer web in the shape of a . . .

Rectangle.

Whoosh! went the wind
and it blew the web away.

Walter sighed. Then he stretched his legs
and made a taller web in the shape of a . . .

Diamond.

Whoosh! Whoosh! went the wind and it blew that web away too!

Perhaps my webs should be more round, thought Walter.

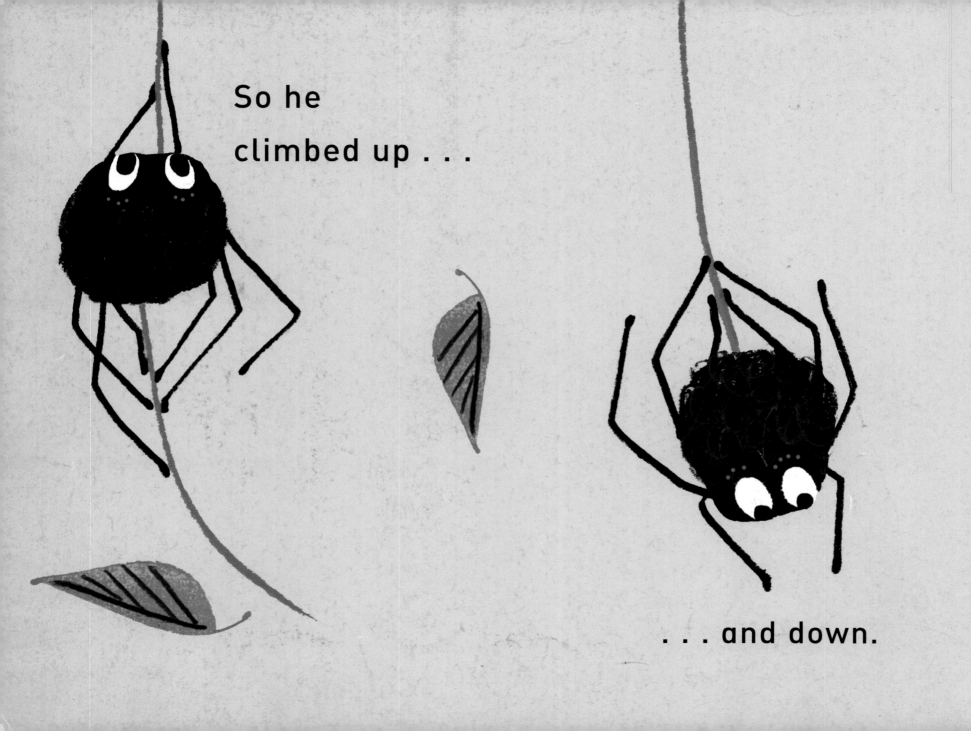

So he

climbed up . . .

. . . and down.

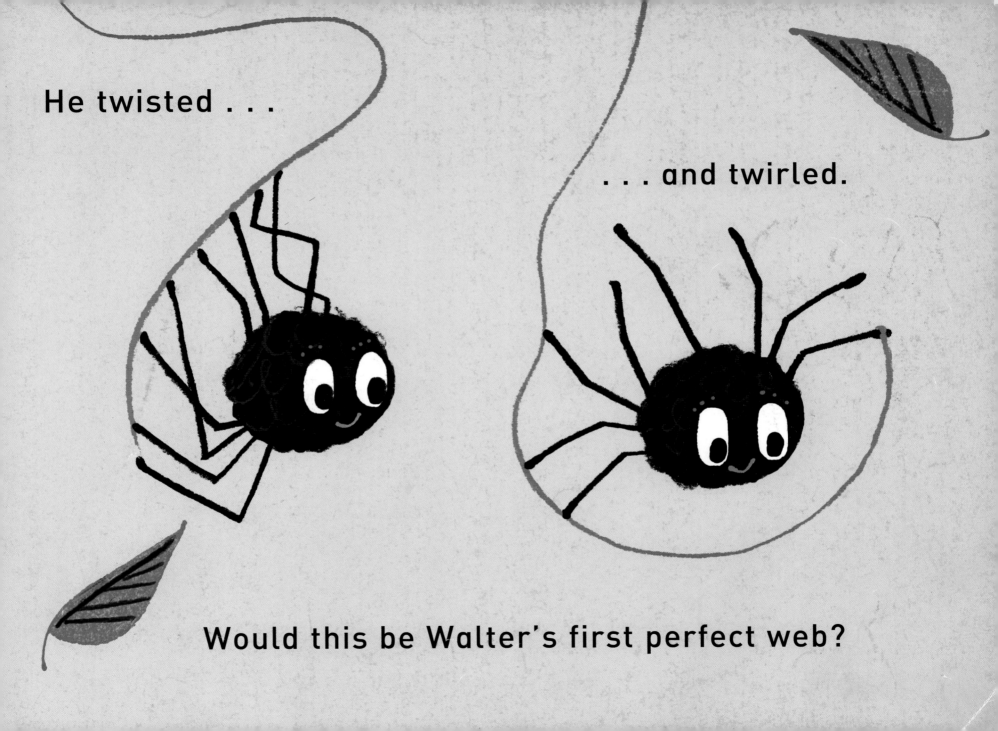

He twisted . . .

. . . and twirled.

Would this be Walter's first perfect web?

Nearly! It wasn't a perfect web, but it was an almost perfect . . .

Circle!

And it looked strong.

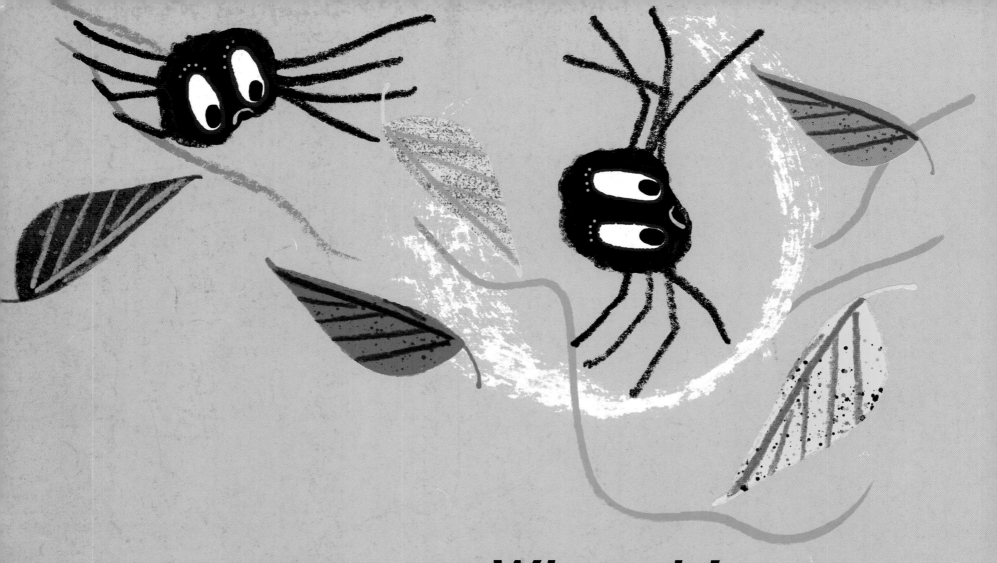

Whoosh! Whoosh! Whoosh!

went the wind.

Poor Walter hit the ground with a **bump**.

Walter was tired and upset.

He felt like giving up.

But as the sun went down,

he thought about all the

different shapes he had made.

All at once, he knew just what to do.

So he took a deep breath and set to work . . .

Whoosh!

went the wind . . .

But it didn't stop Walter,
or his web. Not this time.

And as the stars came out . . .

. . . Walter's web shone
in the moonlight.

It was better than perfect,
it was a truly **wonderful** web!

These basic **shapes** are all shown in this book.

Which shape is a **triangle**?
How many sides does a triangle have?

Which shape is a **square**?
How many sides does a square have?

Which shape is a **rectangle**?
How many sides does a rectangle have?

Which shape is a **diamond**?
How many sides does a diamond have?

Which shape is a **circle**?
Does a circle have any sides?